BENEATH BLAIR MOUNTAIN
Shannon Barnsley

Copyright © 2015 by Shannon Barnsley

ISBN-13: 978-0692566770
ISBN-10: 0692566775

Edited by Rebecca Johnson
Artwork by Mariya Suzuki

Printed in the U.S.A.

BLACK HILL PRESS
blackhillpress.com

Black Hill Press is a publishing collective founded on collaboration. Our growing family of writers and artists are dedicated to the novella—a distinctive, often overlooked literary form that offers the focus of a short story and the scope of a novel. We believe a great story is never defined by its length.

Our independent press produces uniquely curated collections of Contemporary American Novellas. We also celebrate innovative paperback projects with our Special Editions series. Books are available in both print and digital formats, online and in your local bookstore, library, museum, university gift shop, and selected specialty accounts. Discounts are available for book clubs and teachers.

Novellas
1. Corrie Greathouse, *Another Name for Autumn*
2. Ryan Gattis, *The Big Drop: Homecoming*
3. Jon Frechette, *The Frontman*
4. Richard Gaffin, *Oneironautics*
5. Ryan Gattis, *The Big Drop: Impermanence*
6. Alex Sargeant, *Sci-Fidelity*
7. Veronica Bane, *Mara*
8. Kevin Staniec, *Begin*
9. Arianna Basco, *Palms Up*
10. Douglas Cowie, *Sing for Life: Tin Pan Alley*
11. Tomas Moniz, *Bellies and Buffalos*
12. Brett Arnold, *Avalon, Avalon*
13. Douglas Cowie, *Sing for Life: Away, You Rolling River*

Special Editions

SUMMER WRITING PROJECT 2015

Black Hill Press and JukePop are collaborating with the Santa Clara County Library District and California Public Libraries to advocate writing and support reading with their Summer Writing Project (SWP).

Both Black Hill Press and JukePop champion two abandoned mediums. Black Hill Press fights for the novella—a distinctive, often overlooked literary form that offers the focus of a short story and the scope of a novel, while JukePop is rejuvenating the lost art of the serial, pioneered at the dawn of publishing, when authors such as Charles Dickens received critical acclaim and feedback from mass audiences by serializing novels a chapter at a time.

This joint venture presents authors with the opportunity to craft their novellas a chapter at a time with immediate quantitative and qualitative feedback from their readers, while also broadcasting their words to an audience eager for the next great storyteller.

After reading and reviewing our finalists, we selected three novellas to be published as our special Summer Writing Project 2015 collection: *A Stalled Ox* by Dean Moses, *Beneath Blair Mountain* by Shannon Barnsley, and *Let's Stalk Rex Jupiter* by Allison A. Spector. Mariya Suzuki illustrated the cover artwork for this collection.

Visit http://1888.center/swp/ for more information.

JUKEPOP
jukepop.com

JukePop is a social incubation platform that combines
community driven feedback and data analytics to help
authors turn their concepts into great books. We believe
there's at least one great book in every author, the difference
is in how the story is told.

October 30th, 1919, Boston

I kept running. Night was falling, though it barely changed a thing. Boston was grey by day and darker grey by night. The temperature was dropping. It was late October, not the time to find myself homeless again.

They'd long since stopped chasing me, of that I was sure. But what else was I supposed to do? I had nowhere to go and no one in the world left to call my own. Cavan was in the back of a paddy wagon somewhere, Kate was six feet underground (or would have been if there was room enough in the cramped graveyards of New York City), Barrow was likely just a scattering of anonymous buttons and bones left on some godforsaken battlefield a world away, and God only knew what had become of my family.

And if he did, it would certainly be the first time God had taken any notice of the Breckens, or any of the poor souls in Logan County.

A man stopped cursing at his broken down automobile long enough to call out to me as I ran by. Perhaps he did really want to make sure I was okay, but I'd learned long ago not to trust anyone I didn't know (and to keep a weather eye on the ones I did, just to be sure).

I tore past him, bumping into an Italian man who seemed to speak no word of English but "Chicago?" As if by repeating it enough he could will himself there. A woman screamed at her children from behind a small, broken window, filmed over with so much grime that the shattered glass seemed an improvement.

Four blocks over, my searing ribs made me stop. My lungs were raw with cold and nearly ten years of soot and smoke. It felt like a hand was gripping my chest and squeezing the life from me.

I put a hand out to support myself against a brick facade for a moment. I panted. A man in dark clothes was eyeing me from across the street. He saw me looking back and mouthed something.

It was just in my head, I knew. No one was after me. Who was I to anyone anyway? Did the coppers really think Cavan had told me anything of use?

The man was moving towards me.

"You!" he cried out.

My eyes darted about a moment ahead of my feet, searching for any escape. I could barely breathe, let alone outrun an able-bodied man. A barred entrance to the T caught my eye. It was boarded up, allegedly awaiting maintenance, but the thick layer of dust over the sign spoke of a long wait.

"You! It's you," the man cried again. "Wait. I know you. Stop!"

I flew to the barred gateway underground and leapt through a space between the boards. It was longer down than through and my balance was off, sending me tumbling down stone stair after stone stair. I hit my legs, hip, and ribs on the way down. Broken bottles no doubt thrown through by passing drunks tore at me like briars as I fell.

I hit my head at the bottom. For a moment I saw lights in the darkness, bursts of green dancing across my eyes. My head swam and I feared the dark would take me. Instead, I managed to half-turn myself to the side and wretch. My bones protested as I pulled myself up to a sitting position. I could feel the bruises that would flower tomorrow, but I had long ago stopped counting on tomorrow.

Thin as I was, I had barely made it through, so unless the man could pull the boards loose, there was no chance of him following me down. That is, even if he had seen me go in. Still, that cut off the only way out for now. Who knew if there was another, let alone one I could find in the dark before tripping or walking off the subway platform. And it was colder down here.

Even if I managed to explore the place in my sorry, battered state without breaking my neck, I might freeze to death before finding my way out. Boston falls were more like West Virginia winters and I hadn't a patched coat to my name. I hadn't anything to my name now, though that was far from a first. I wrapped my arms around my chest, my thin, torn sleeves wet with blood from the bottles' unexpected wrath. The blood felt warm on my skin. For now, at least.

I took a breath, trying to quell the panic that had been pumping through my veins since they'd come for Cavan. However, that only left a sinking feeling that threatened to overwhelm me. I was going to die down here. I could push back the fear all I liked, but that didn't make it any less likely that this abandoned T station could very well be my tomb.

Still, it wasn't like I'd be the first Brecken to be swallowed up by the earth.

Spring 1910, Logan County, West Virginia

To say I grew up in a dirt poor town is as true as it gets. Not even the dirt belonged to us. The land, the town, the mine, it all belonged to the coal company. We lived in company houses, prayed in company churches, learned in company schools, and were beaten by company police officers when we thought too hard about it. But it wasn't always bad.

Sometimes there was a wedding or a christening or a rare holiday. Then everyone would put on their Sunday best (or, in the case of the Lachey family, whatever they could patch together of what had once been the Sunday best of near half the town). The women would get gussied up and fuss over the children, determined that no one could pity their brood tonight.

The men would shave and strip themselves of the roughness of the mines and the woodstove and the wood still needing to be chopped. The house would smell of shaving cream and warm apple pie as the women all swarmed like locusts, yet somehow left a feast in their wake instead of devouring one.

All the day before the women would congregate in the kitchen, drawing more and more female relatives and neighbors in like wise men to the manger. Though, as they cackled over pots, stirred bubbling broths, sacrificed turkeys, and somehow magicked scraps into feasts, I wondered if perhaps they were more a gathering of witches than pilgrims.

In the kitchen together, with no menfolk to bother them, they let their hair down for perhaps the only time since they'd become wives or elder sisters. They'd laugh and gossip and swat little hands trying to secret away a hunk of Butcher's Blood cornbread before the festivities started.

Then, after all the preparation, the fun would begin. Homer Barrow would take up his grandfather's fiddle and the Pritchett boy would bring out the washboard as the preacher's girls or the school teacher's good for nothing nephew would take up the tune. Together they lent their voices to all those who'd gone before, whether they were silenced like a songbird down in the mines or died rasping their last confession out of lungs far blacker than their souls.

The couples would dance and the boys would size up the young ladies. Though, in a few years' time all of them would become indistinguishable from their weary mothers, their fingers worn from washing and trying to rub together two pennies they'd never had to start with. Still, in those moments, everyone was convinced that Rose and Ethel Gibson or Myrtle Kagy would go on looking like the perfect china dolls they were for all time, even if Mrs. Gibson and the late Mrs. Kagy had once been just as lovely.

Sometimes the old people told stories. Ancient ones, from their grandpap's grandpap's grandpap. The kind folks elsewhere called "from back home" in "the old country." While the rest of America was grappling over what to call themselves, what language to speak at home, what flag to raise, and what to do when their children rejected their hope chests of traditional clothing for a clean suit and the promise of more, we had no such qualms. We knew exactly who we were. And we knew we'd never get any more.

The people here had long since become something new, our roots as deep as the mine, our origins more and more untraceable with every generation that passed. Were the Gibsons really Portuguese as they now claimed or Shawnee Indians as their grandfather had? And how come the Massies were white when their cousins the McNabbs were paler than the lot of them and everyone knew their great-grandparents had been slaves. Was the school teacher's good for nothing nephew really descended from Jacobite rebels or did he just say that to get his Protestant uncle's color up?

And what were we Breckens? We used to be called Irish until the real Irish started coming over. No one wanted to throw our lot in with them, though Uncle Jim didn't really see a whole lot of difference in dying for the railroads or dying for the coal that powered them. But Ma, Pa, and Aunt Betsy didn't want anyone mistaking us for those Catholic hooligans, so they had dropped the word "Irish" like a hot potato.

Now we called ourselves Scotch-Irish, but that wasn't the whole truth either. There was definitely a smattering of Italian and maybe a Cherokee or two in the family tree. And whatever other secrets my freckled olive skin told.

Even if we weren't real Irish though, that's where the stories came from. Stories of the Tuatha De Danann, the original inhabitants of Ireland, who'd gone to war with the newcomers to the land, only to sign a treaty when victory slipped from their hands. The new Irish would get the surface of Ireland and the no-longer-Irish, now called fey folk, would get what lay beneath. That was where fairyland was, my grandmother told me.

As a child, I tried and tried to picture fairyland. I'd shut my eyes tight and try to picture girls prettier than the Gibson sisters twirling in dresses spun by spiders from their finest silks. I'd try to smell the sweetmeats and tarts oozing berries like old blood and imagine fairer folk than we eating finer food than I would ever taste. Folks who would never know hunger, even as their conquerors pulled nothing but blight and famine from the ground.

I'd try to imagine music that would lead me astray, stumbling through the moors in a blind fervor like the Shakers when they go to their funny churches, but all I heard was Barrow's fiddle, his winks leading me into more temptation than any fey song. I hoped elf-churches were more lenient on the matter of tempting winks and boys who smelled like earth and woodsmoke (and knew how to draw bows across wooden curves just right to make them sing) than the Shakers. Or our church, for that matter.

I'd try to picture an underground realm of exile, sometimes a heavenly refuge and sometimes a hell for the forgotten people of a land that left them behind. I'd try to imagine the chasms that opened up and swallowed stolen children whole, young people lured into servitude and death by silvered promises on honeyed lips. I'd try to picture the caves that led down into fairyland or, in some stories, into hell itself, but all I could see was the mine.

October 30th, 1919, Boston

I forced myself to stand. I could stay here, hoping that my pursuer would move on and I could sneak back up, assuming of course I could get back through the boards from a lower angle and with no running start. Or I could press on and look for another way out.

I took a few steps away from where the waning light of day cast into the twilight of the abandoned subway platform. My leg fell out from beneath me and I went down. I landed in a heap. My ankle screamed.

I reached down to my foot. My well-worn boot had finally given out, the heel having popped off entirely. I eased the patched remains of the boot off. My ankle wasn't swollen yet, but it smarted like a switch. Hopefully it was only twisted and not broken. Still, that didn't leave me a lot of options.

I pulled the small box of matches from my pocket. Lucifers, my grandmother had called them. I'd been lighting the gas when they came for Cavan and they were all I had a chance to bring. There were six left.

I struck one and a warm orange glow filled the gloomy underground. I could just make out the edges of the platform. A beady-eyed creature skittered across the tracks below, squeaking at the sudden light.

I looked around but found only cobwebs and old crates. Whenever it was that this station broke down, it certainly wasn't recent and they seemed in no hurry to get it back up and running.

I swore as the flame burned my fingers. Ma always told me not to sound so common. But the truth is I'm as common as it gets. Girls like me are everywhere. In Logan County, in New York City, in Boston. Some olive-skinned like me; some black; some brown; some pale like my best friend Kate, God rest her soul; some every color in between. We're everywhere.

And nobody gives a damn about us anywhere on this ashen heap we call the earth. Old World or New World, it'll never be our world. The most we can do is cling to some godforsaken corner of it until we die, and perhaps live long enough to leave equally desperate girls behind.

First order of business was the matter of my shoes. I couldn't very well hobble about with one heel. And with all the glass and rats and God knows what else down here, I couldn't very well prance around in stocking feet like a child on a winter's morning. I tore strips of cloth from the hem of my dress and ripped off my torn and useless sleeves. I wobbled, trying to remove my other shoe and wrapped up my feet in the cloth. It would have to do for now.

I struck another match and began to slowly edge my way about the platform, careful to keep the drop at least an arm's distance from me. The floor was littered in broken bottles and the occasional subway coin but nothing much else. There was no other exit. I guessed the people who built it had just had to hope there would never be a fire.

It didn't surprise me, though. Eight years ago they could leave us in cloth-strewn tinder boxes with locked doors and no exits. Things had begun to change, but change never moves as quickly as it should and forgotten corners like old T stations and dirt poor towns in Logan County were always bound to follow much slower. Or miss out on change entirely as the rest of the world moved on without them, cobwebs in the corner of a growing nation.

The flame went out in a sudden gust. My hair stood on the back of my neck. Much like when Mr. Williams would "observe" us girls working back in my factory days, the feeling that I wasn't alone, that I was being watched, slithered down my spine like cold wash water.

Of course, it was just the fears of a hysterical girl. No one else could possibly be down here. I was completely alone, except for the rats.

That's when I tripped over something and felt myself pitch forward, reeling in the darkness. I put out my arms to break my fall and my elbow and palm slammed into the hard stone floor, skinning both. I reached for a match to see what the devil I had tripped on. It felt like a tree root. I turned, half-scrambling up into a squat, and found myself staring into the faces of the dead.

Summer 1910, Logan County, West Virginia

It was summer, hot and humid and oppressive. It was also the summer I would have married Homer Barrow. Sure, I was young and he was hell-bent on getting out of Logan County to make it as a musician. We were fools, the both of us, everyone said. No one outside Appalachia would pay to listen to "Mountain music" and no one in Appalachia could. How on earth would a fiddler support a family, they wondered, even with a real woman at his side instead of a silly girl like Lara Rae Brecken?

But then Barrow's pa went and broke his leg down in the mine and couldn't work. Barrow had brothers, but they were older and had their own families to support. So Barrow, who played the fiddle as fine as any elf-lord I could imagine, went down into the earth.

His smiles disappeared and his fiddle gathered dust as the boy I knew transformed into some gaunt creature with the same name. He started using harsh words with his mother and had no time for me. After his best friend, Harry

McNabb, died in a cave-in, he started going to meetings. The kind that got you fired. And in our little speck of dirt poor earth in Logan County, employer-owned houses were for employees.

Homer, his wailing ma, and his crippled pa were turned out of their house. His brothers blamed him, but only one of them offered to take the three homeless Barrows in. However, it turned out to be a lighter burden than Emmett Barrow and his wife, Mary Beth Barrow (née McNabb), expected. The next morning Mr. Barrow was found reeking of whiskey and dead by his own hand on the old hanging tree. Homer Barrow left town after that but not before stopping at my house.

He said he couldn't make good on his promise to make an honest woman of me, but he could get me as far as New York. He was going to sell his fiddle to get away. One look at my family was all I needed.

Six screaming children. My poor Ma working her fingers to the bone to feed us all since the black lung took Pa. My brother, Johnnie, who had aged ten years in the four months he'd been in the mines. My eldest sister, Elizabeth, not three years older, with two screaming children of her own and a husband who found more solace in the bottom of a bottle (or Myrtle Kagy) than he did in her.

Aunt Betsy and Johnnie screamed that no kin of theirs was going to be a working girl up North, living God knows where with God knows who, letting Yankee boys do God knows what to me to make rent. Ma and Elizabeth were quiet. They didn't want me to go, but it'd mean whatever money I could spare sent back home if I did. It meant one less mouth to feed and one less back to clothe.

So, one grey morning I left with Barrow. I walked past his empty house and the church and the schoolhouse and the mist-shrouded shadow of Blair Mountain. All of it the coal company's. I got on a train, choking on the smell of burning coal (no doubt also the coal company's). And I didn't look back until we reached New York City.

October 30th, 1919, Boston

I backed away in horror, cutting my hand on a shard of broken glass as I did. The dead woman stared blankly back at me. Her once-black hair shone in the match light, half-obscured by a dusty scarf. Her cheeks, undoubtedly hallow even when she'd been alive, were pools of shadow beneath flame lit cheekbones.

She lay slumped against the wall. No doubt she'd sought shelter down in here as I had and never left. Likely froze to death. She must have been an immigrant. Her tattered clothes looked Eastern European in origin, though I couldn't for the life of me say what kind exactly. I could tell they had been beautiful once, all intricate patterns and brocades. I wondered if her mother had made them for her, a piece of home she could still claim and wrap herself up in when America had proved no warmer. If so, she had died richer than I.

The woman was not alone. In her arms was a small bundle that had once been a baby, a tuft of black hair and a small, withered hand were all that showed through the swaddled lump of moth-eaten fabric. Tucked at the woman's side was a small child, a girl. The woman's shawl was still wrapped around them both.

The little girl's blonde hair shone in the light. I wondered why the woman had not sold it to a wig-maker if they were indeed desperate enough to die here, tattered and starving and cold. Of course, I suppose someone could wonder the same of me. Perhaps the girl's spun gold locks were more in vogue, but my hair was the kind of sleek black sheen not often seen outside of Appalachia or an Indian reservation. I probably should have sold it. It might have kept the wolves at bay when I was on the street. Though perhaps a shorn sheep would have been no safer.

The light flickered out and the three ill-fated souls vanished before me.

I struck another match. I was burning through my light all too quickly, but the woman looked about my size and I would need better outfitting if I was to survive. With a murmured word of apology I gently undid the woman's boots and slipped them on, wincing both for my ankle and my hesitation at stealing from the dead. The boots pinched my toes a bit when I stood but nothing I hadn't endured wearing my sister's hand-me-downs. Letting out one last breath of reservation, I gently pulled the woman's shawl from behind her and the girl.

A chill went through me even as I wrapped myself in the warmth of worn wool. The light was running low, my fifth match. I hurried to the edge of the platform. Careful not to cut myself again, I placed a large piece of broken glass on the ground with the cloth wrappings I no longer needed for my feet on top. In the last moment of light, I dropped the match

—

on the cloth. It went up in seconds. I had to take a breath to push back memories of the day Kate died. The cloth was burning quickly. Now was my only chance.

If I stayed on the platform I would die like the foreign woman and her children. If I followed the tracks I would either find a way out or get flattened along the way, the rats picking clean whatever was left. Why bother to be afraid, though? That was essentially what I'd been doing my whole life.

Trying not to think of trains or rats, I lowered myself down off the platform. My feet still dangled about a foot above the surface below, so I had to let go and fall. I cried out as my ankle gave way beneath me and I once again hit the ground. Splinters stung my arm as the rotten wood greeted me at the bottom. I sputtered earth and grit and limped to my feet. My ankle protested against the weight, but I willed myself to stand and take a step. The light grew dim above me.

With one match left I would have to go in darkness. If I kept my hand to the wall, though, and kept going forward, I wouldn't lose my way, even without a flame to guide me. It was certainly no darker than the mine so many of my kin had died in. I was Lara Rae Brecken of Logan County, daughter to miners as far back as there were mines in West Virginia. I could do this.

The light went out. I choked on fear thick as molasses as my heart beat cold blood into my veins. Never in my life had I felt so very alone.

Fall 1910, New York City

"Dinner is at six o'clock and lights out is at eight. It should go without saying, but it seems these days it bears mentioning that no gentlemen callers are welcome after curfew," the wizened old woman said, glaring at me and Barrow as though we were running naked through the streets on Easter Sunday.

"That won't be a problem, ma'am," I said with a stone-steady look at Barrow. "I have no gentleman callers."

"Good. You'd be wise to keep it that way, Miss Brecken," Madam O'Keefe continued. "My aunt Brigid worked in a home for unwed mothers back in Dublin and all the girls there had been convinced their lads had loved them. Sworn up and down they'd marry them, they did. Yet there they were: no husband to speak of and a babe on the way with no means to feed or clothe it. Idiot girls, the lot of them.

"And don't think for a moment the swill those shady adverts sell will help you a wink. I've seen girls die that way all too easy and it's illegal, you know. They only get away with it because the police are too plum foolish to know what the papers mean when they hawk pills and potions for 'female complaints' and 'lunar regularity'. Damned fools the lot of 'em. That shite's like enough to be poison as medicine."

The woman droned on about the various perils of lustful ways and young men who never did make good on their promises to marry so long I thought I might scream. Barrow's face was pale with guilt, but that made me feel no better. He was still leaving me here.

"There are fourteen girls here, counting yourself, Miss Brecken," she told me. "Some don't speak much English and most keep to themselves. We have two Lauras already though, so we'll have to call you something else. Do you have a middle name?"

"My name isn't Laura," I told her. "It's Lara."

"What's the difference?"

I blinked, at a loss for words. "One isn't..." I murmured. "I'm Lara. Lara Rae. After my grandmother Lorelei and my mother's dearest friend Rae Ann."

"What kind of a name is Lorelei?" the woman asked. "Sounds like a strumpet putting on airs. Very well, Laura May it is then."

"Lara Rae," I insisted.

But Madam O'Keefe paid me no mind. She pushed open the door to a small room with one bed and a trunk at its foot.

"You'll be in with Catherine Brannon. She's at work now. Works over at the garment factory in the Asch building, she does. She's a good girl, though that lad of hers will do her no good. Anyway, I'll let you get settled. You'll have to bid Mr. Barrow farewell now-"

"Actually, ma'am, I'd like a moment with L- with Miss Brecken if you would," Barrow said.

Madam O'Keefe's face pinched as though she had tasted something sour.

"I'd like to help her settle in," Barrow continued. "And I have something for her. From her mother."

"Really, Mr. Barrow, I must insist-"

Barrow drew himself up to his full height. He'd slouched ever since he'd taken up work in the mine.

"No, Madam O'Keefe, I really must insist. We've paid for her room and it's nowhere near past curfew, so I'll thank you to take your head out of the gutter for a moment. I would like to say goodbye to my childhood friend who is very dear to me, something I'm sure no man this side of madness has ever said of you." He took my hand, pulling me into the room. "Now good day, Madam."

"But-"

"I said good day," he growled, slamming the door shut in her pinched face.

Once inside I threw my arms around Barrow, kissing him as I hadn't since before he went down into the mines. He returned it with equal passion, his rough hands holding me as I never imagined they would again. My small bundle of things fell to the floor with a thump I'm sure Madam O'Keefe heard. His lips were on my neck. Heat flushed through me as a small noise escaped my own lips. Though I dearly wished not to, I pulled away.

"Mister Barrow," I chided. "You should not have said such things to my new landlady. I do have to live with her after you leave."

"I didn't like the way she was speaking to you," he said. "Lorelei is a beautiful name and she's no right to cast doubts on my Lara."

"But I'm not your Lara, am I?" I asked, sitting down on the bed.

It was rock hard and uneven. I'd have slept better on the side of Blair Mountain. I'd have breathed better there too. The city was as soot-stained as the men of Logan County after the last whistle sent them home for supper. And it smelled just as foul.

"Lara..." Barrow began, taking my hands as he knelt before me. "I told you. I'm joining the Army. I'll be gone. You can't come with me and I won't have much to send you if I'm already sending half my pay back home to my family-"

"You don't owe them-"

"Yes," he cut me off. "I do."

I stared at the floor.

"Besides, nice homes like this only take unmarried girls who send their money back home to their families. You'll be far safer and happier here than in whatever hovel you could get as a married woman with no husband around."

I nodded. Salt burned my eyes like my grandmother said it did the fairies.

"I can't promise I'll come back for you and I'm sorry for that," he told me. "I'm sorry we couldn't get married in the summer like I promised and I don't want to break another promise to you. But I do love you, Lara Rae Brecken. You're my first love. My first..." he trailed off. "You'll always be in my heart, Lara. No matter where I go. And I can promise this: if you're in trouble, if you are mistreated here or at work or anywhere else and you need help, you write to me and I'll be there."

"You won't be there. You'll be with the Army."

"I'll get help somehow or I'll find a way to get to you. I'll say my mother is sick. I'll desert if I have to."

"I thought you said you didn't want to break another promise," I said, picking at a stray thread on the thin quilt beneath me.

"I love you, Lara," he said again. "I'm sorry to leave you, but I have to. If you love me still and I know you do-"

"I don't."

"What?" His hands went slack over mine.

I looked down at him, my grey eyes as cold as he had been these past few months. "I loved the boy with the fiddle who smiled and played music for me."

That cut him more deeply than I intended, his fiddle still like a missing limb to him. It wasn't just the one thing he loved doing, it had been his grandfather's and his before him, brought over from Ireland when Barrow's own Scotch-Irish ancestors had left their tenant farm for a better life in America.

He let go of my hands, sinking to the floor. "You don't mean that."

"I do."

"You're not a cruel girl like Myrtle, Lara. I know you."

"You knew the girl who liked fairy stories and fell for a fiddler's promises." I got up from the bed, blinking away tears. I retrieved the bundle from the floor. "Now, if you'll excuse me, I have to unpack."

"Lara, don't-"

At that moment the door opened. A girl stood in the doorway, eyes wide. She was a pretty girl through the fatigue that clung to her pale face. Near everyone I knew back home had pale grey eyes like me or else brown ones. Hers were a foggy green, her hair as rust red as mine was coal black.

"I suppose you must be Laura then," she said, her eyes darting from me to the man on our bedroom floor. "And this is?"

"Homer Barrow," he said, having recovered enough to rise and offer her a hand. "I'm Lara Rae's... friend from back home. Could we just have a moment?"

"No need," I said, standing. "Homer was just leaving."

He shot me a look.

"Mustn't keep the Army waiting," I told him.

"Just. Just promise you'll write," he nearly begged.

"Fine," I snapped.

He swooped in for a hug I did not return and a kiss on the cheek that jolted me. Then with a nod to my new roommate he was gone.

"Lara then, not Laura?" my roommate asked.

I nodded, trying to hold back the tears. "You're- you're Catherine Brannon?" My voice broke.

"Kate," she said. "Or Katie. Do you want to talk about it, Lara?"

I shook my head. The tears already spilling down my face. I sank back down onto the bed. Kate was beside me in a moment, her arm around me as she drew me to her as though I were a beloved sister.

"Shhhh, Lara," she said, "It's okay. I cried when I first came here too. The first night I missed my mother so badly I cried until Olga pounded on my door to let her sleep."

I began to half-sob my woes: Pa dying, Harry McNabb dying down in the mine, Barrow spurning me, his father hanging himself, leaving my family, everything. She held me all the while and listened.

By evening she was braiding my hair as she spoke of her own family, who had come here from Galway with nothing

October 30th, 1919, Boston

I pulled the shawl tighter about me and took a step. My ankle seared. I took another. And another and another and another. My hand never left the cool stone wall. It was slow-going, but I kept going all the same.

Eventually I would have to come out at another station. I kept myself alert for any hint of light or a breeze or any sense of change. There was nothing but the skittering of rats and the sound of my hand tracing the wall. As the shooting pain in my ankle crept up my leg into my knee, my legs grew stiff and tired.

I began to hear a voice. Soft and lilting and far away. It seemed almost to be singing, but the words were in a language I had only overheard in hushed tones while Cavan did business.

"Hello?" I called out. The empty tunnel echoed back.

Again I heard the voice. This time I knew it was a man. I still could not make out the words, but they were English now. An Irishman, to be sure. He was calling to me, asking me for help.

"Hello?" I asked again. "Did you say 'help me'?"

"Help me. Help me. Help me," cried either the Irishman or my own voice somewhere in the cavernous black void.

"Are you in here?" I shouted.

"Here! Here! Here!" the cries seemed to come from all around.

I felt for it. My last match. Was some other vagrant worth it? And how had he come to be down here anyway? Drunk like as not. Why should I waste my last match on him? Lord knew there were enough of him above ground to be getting on with.

But all I saw was Kate and Cavan, both crying out forever in my mind, an eternal loop of people I couldn't help. I saw Barrow dying on the battlefield, a new, more gruesome death each time. Had anyone tried to save him? Or had the other soldiers just kept going. What was one poor Yank to them (though only an Englishman or a Frenchman would call him that)?

I saw the faces of all the people who had walked past me on the streets and looked away. I wasn't their kin, not their kind. Why should they waste their hard-earned money on some homeless hillbilly?

I struck the match.

The man lay crumpled facedown across the tracks before me. I ran to him and turned him over only to find a skeleton in his clothes. I backed away. He was dead. Long dead. Long enough that these tracks couldn't still be in use. I choked down fear that I had gone the wrong way and now would die in even blacker darkness in a deeper grave than the woman I'd robbed.

I shook. He couldn't have been the one I heard. It must have been an echo. But I'd heard singing. I'd heard someone speaking. I'd heard Irish. I was sure of it.

The man had a swag bag on him. Inside was an old photograph of a wife and four children back in Ireland. There were clothes that fell near to dust when unfolded. Some chewing tobacco. A bottle of something that had curdled away. And a box of matches. I eagerly tore it open and then leapt back.

Those weren't the same as the match I now held all too close to the box. They were white phosphorus matches. Dangerous. Volatile. Their poison heads once a suicide of choice. They were illegal in every decent country but ours, though at least they'd fallen out of favor and factory workers had stopped dying from handling them all day.

Still, when I was cast back into shadow with the corpse and the ghosts and the sound of my own blood hammering in my ears, I didn't care how deadly they were. The damn Lucifers were my last hope of salvation.

Winter 1911, New York City

Ma wrote to me, thanking me for the money I'd sent her and warning me not to trust anyone, lest I end up like those poor girls at the World's Fair or those prostitutes in London. I kept telling her those cases were ancient and no serial killer was operating within the confines of Madam O'Keefe's Home for Young Women, but she worried all the same.

The other girls in the building were a mix of newly arrived immigrants and small town girls sent off to the city to work when suitable husbands had not been left at the door with the day's milk and eggs. Despite never having set foot outside Logan County until a few months before, I felt myself relating more to the newcomers to America than to my own countrymen. I guess New York City is a long way from West Virginia in more ways than one. The American girls judged my out of date clothes and funny accent as much as they did the Polish, Italian, and German girls in the house.

But I was never wanting for company. Kate and her family friend—now fiancé—Cavan Neely had found me a job at the Triangle Shirtwaist Factory. It was tedious work in a sweltering, cloth-strewn prison of a room nine hours a day (seven on Saturday), but we made the best of it. It was mostly young women there, some still learning English.

Our table, piled high with scraps, was made up of me, Kate, Hannah Zalensky, Battista Fattore, Gitl Baumann, and Mary Donahue. At first Gitl and Mary had thought me Italian like Battista; Hannah had thought I was a gypsy; and Battista had asked half in fear, half in awe if I was "Indiana," though I'm still not sure if she meant the kind whose graves we'd built our homes over or the kind under British rule.

When I explained I was Scotch-Irish and Protestant, Mary edged away and whispered something sharp to Kate in a tongue Kate barely understood and could no longer speak. For the first time, I was the "other" in a place where having your own kind at your back was the only way to survive. Perhaps we Breckens would have been better off throwing in our lot with those "Catholic hooligans" after all, even if it would have labeled us "off-white."

Kate and Cavan's acceptance eventually warmed Mary to me, though, and the girls and I would laugh our way through the long hours to earn our seven dollars a month. At night we would bid farewell, Cavan would head off to workers' meetings (the kind that had gotten Barrow fired), and Kate and I would hurry home to scarf down dinner and whisper our secrets under a shared quilt at night. I knew she and Cavan would be happy together, but I dreaded their marriage, knowing it meant she would leave the boarding house.

That dreaded prospect never came to pass, though. Life had a far crueler twist in mind one dreary, miserable day in March. The sky was grey as Kate and I hurried to work, getting chastised by Mr. Williams for being two minutes late. We settled in with the girls and tried to warm ourselves with smiles and whispers, our comradeship never quite enough to keep the cold at bay.

The morning wore on and afternoon inched by just as it always did: Battista whispering naughty English words she'd learned and giggling, Cavan always finding a reason to drop by and see us. Mary would throw a barb his way, saying Mr. Williams would be hiring again soon. Cavan's sole duty seemed to be overseeing us, so surely they'd soon hire a man for each table. Hannah would then elbow her in the ribs, more than happy for more time spent looking at Cavan.

Her schoolgirl infatuation never bothered Kate, though. Kate wasn't a jealous person and there was no way Hannah's family would even consider letting her marry out. Besides, in addition to being one of the few men at Triangle Shirtwaist, Cavan was one of even fewer who actually cared about any of us. All of the women on the floor were more than happy when he was supervising us, even if he did make the gaggle two tables over stop sneaking puffs of Widow Koch's cigarette.

It was Saturday. We just had to get through the rest of the day and then tomorrow was our day off. Battista and Hannah chattered on about their plans for the day. Gitl and I both could think only of a nap. Kate had her mother's veil to fix up for the wedding.

After Cavan came by the third time that day, the needle on my machine snapped. I went to the back room to grab a new one. My neck pricked its own needles. Mr. Williams appeared behind me.

"Stealing supplies, are we?" he asked.

The door was so close, but I couldn't get back out with him standing there. I tried to edge sideways. "Just getting a new needle, Mr. Williams. Mine broke."

"Again?" He put out an arm to block the door further. "That's the third time, Lana."

"Lara," I said.

It wasn't completely true. The first time Battista had broken hers and had been short on results the day before. She'd been so afraid of being fired that she'd broken down crying, so I swapped needles with her. She'd thanked me over and over that day and brought a basket of her mother's Italian baking round to the boarding house that Sunday.

"Don't be smart with me, missy." He rushed forward and grabbed my arm. "You're a thief and you're stealing from the supplies."

"I didn't-"

"Liar," he growled. His grip tightened on my arm.

"I weren't lying," I told him, trying to pull my arm away. "And I ain't no thief, sir. I just broke my needle." Maybe if he didn't buy cheap machines the needles wouldn't keep breaking.

"I could fire you for this," he said. "You were late today too. I probably should."

My heart was beating like a rabbit's in a snare. He shut the door.

"Though, perhaps I could be lenient. For such an...accommodating worker." His free hand stroked my other arm. "Lara, was it?"

I recoiled as if burned, tearing myself loose. I held the needle in my hand. I couldn't do much damage with it, but maybe I could do enough to get by and run...where? The doors were locked so we couldn't take breaks or slip away to rifle through the stock. I couldn't leave the ninth floor without someone in charge letting me. Cavan might outrank us girls, but he didn't outrank Mr. Williams yet and he didn't have a key.

"Oh, don't play coy with me," Mr. Williams said, shutting the door. "Pretty girl like you?"

"Sir..."

"You're not like the frigid little virgins out there who wouldn't know what to do with a man if he fell at their feet. Bet you had quite a few rolls in the hay with the mountain men back home. Didn't you?"

"Stay back," I warned.

"You want to keep your job, don't you?" he asked. "Or do your after-hour activities keep you just fine? Bet a girl like you could make a pretty penny that way. Exotic as those foreign girls, but you can actually speak English instead of just nodding like that idiot Italian girl." He took another step towards me. "Course that won't much matter if I do my job right. What do you say, little canary? Think I can make you sing better than those coal miners could?"

The door burst open behind Mr. Williams, knocking him off balance. He spun around. Cavan, brown eyes burning under his auburn hair, punched Mr. Williams square in the jaw.

"You filthy son of a bitch!" he screamed.

Mr. Williams' face had gone slack with shock.

Cavan grabbed him by the collar, shaking him as his face went red with rage. Obscenities flew like bullets. Other girls came running. A few of them saw me standing there and immediately understood. It seemed I was not the first. The rest looked from me to Mr. Williams to Cavan in utter confusion.

Some screamed, thinking Cavan was going to kill Mr. Williams. Eventually, the man from the eighth floor came running up to see what the fuss was and pulled Cavan off of a shrieking Mr. Williams, whose coat was now stained with the blood that was pouring from his nose.

"Neely, I put up with your union talk and your flirting, but you've gone too far," said the man from downstairs.

"Get out!" Mr. Williams screamed. He touched his hand to his bruised face. It came away bloody. "Get out! Both of you!"

"Both?" asked the man.

"Her," Mr. Williams growled, pointing at me. "Get the paddy rabble-rouser and his slut out of here."

I saw his words hit Kate's face like a slap. I tried to make eye contact with her, to somehow explain.

"No!" I screamed. "It was him! I'm a good worker. I do my job. It was him. I weren't doing nothing wrong. I need this job!"

"GET OUT!" Mr. Williams roared.

The man from downstairs began to pull me away. I screamed, shouting incoherently to him, to Cavan, to Kate, to Mr. Williams, even to Battista to say something.

Cavan whispered something to Kate and took my arm much more gently than either of the other men had. "C'mon, Lara. Just come with me."

I followed, my head so light that my body seemed to move on its own. I barely remember the elevator or leaving the building, only then remembering I hadn't yet been paid for this week. Cavan told me to forget it, that I'd never see a penny of it and it'd be worse if I went back.

I was out of my mind with terror. I'd lost my job. Kate no doubt thought I was a loose woman tempting her fiancé.

—

Mr. Williams had tried to force himself on me. And now Kate and Battista and Mary and Hannah and Gitl and all the rest were still in there with him and Cavan wouldn't be there next time. Not to mention Cavan had lost his job, an even better one than mine. How would he support a wife, even if Kate would still have him?

I remember Cavan pulling me away to try to talk me down, but I was shaking even worse now and I couldn't think. My mind was racing and blank all at once. He just kept saying it would be okay. He knew some people who might be able to help. Workers' union people. The kind that had gotten him and Barrow in enough trouble already.

That's when the bale of cotton fell from the window.

I looked to the Asch building that I was now barred from. Triangle Shirtwaist occupied the eighth, ninth, and tenth floors. I could make out two figures at the window. A man and a woman. They were kissing. Then they leapt.

Cavan saw them fall but didn't make out what it was he was seeing. "Why are they dropping cloth down?"

I stood frozen, my blood cold as the air that day.

"It's not cloth," I said. "They're jumping."

Someone else on the street screamed as another body came crashing down to the pavement below. After that it was all screams and panic and madness.

"Fire!" a man screamed. "Fire!"

The windows of the eighth floor bloomed orange.

"They're on the ninth!" I screamed. "Kate! Battista! Hannah! They're on the ninth floor! They're all still up there!"

I tried to run back to the building, but someone grabbed me and held me back. The fire brigade came wailing in. The firemen rushed out, but the bodies kept falling, a human barricade keeping them from the entrance. The ninth floor was burning.

I was screaming. I don't even remember where Cavan was at that point. The streets were a madhouse of horrified on-lookers and the firemen fighting to keep them back just as they fought to get in.

Bodies everywhere. Twisted, bent, arms and legs buckled beneath them, snapped like twigs in a gale. Like how they say the Indians hunted buffalo by chasing them off cliffs, a graveyard of mangled meat on the blood-stained altar below. Yet they kept falling. A rain of girls, swept away from every corner of the world and carried here to New York just to be dashed against the paved ground of a foreign land before their roots were ever planted.

Bones stuck out of torn skin at angles I could never have imagined. Lone shoes lay scattered, black from soot both old and new, and already being scooped up by opportunistic lookers-on. All around me were faces at once too familiar and unrecognizable, now more like the grotesqueries painted on carnival signs than the prim little women in the photographs their loved ones here and abroad would soon clutch in futility.

"There!" Cavan cried. "It's Kate!"

I looked up to see girls rushing out onto the fire escape. I could barely make them out, but Kate's russet hair was clear as day.

"C'mon, Kate," Cavan prayed, barely breathing as he spoke. "C'mon. You can do it. C'mon, Kate."

But the fire was warping the rusted metal, likely broken before any of the girls had stepped out onto it. My heart dropped out as the fire escape swung away from the building and broke, sending the nearly two-dozen girls plummeting down nine floors. I saw Kate, her copper hair a blazing phoenix as she fell. Cavan nearly knocked a firefighter's teeth out and I bit another trying to get by, but it was no use. Kate was dead before we reached her.

Cavan held her shattered body to his own, screaming and crying and cursing in a language beyond words. For a moment I felt light, then I hit concrete beside my fellow workers. At first the firefighters thought me a survivor, but Cavan must have told them I'd fainted.

I floated in and out. I saw Battista and a girl who might have been Hannah. Cavan later said he had seen Gitl arm in arm with another girl from the floor. They never did find Mary. At some point there were coffins on the street. The bodies were moved to where their families could identify them.

But the Brannons would never see Kate's. They were too far away. Instead it was Cavan who claimed her. Cavan who buried her.

I stood next to him at the funeral, wondering if she'd hated me when she died. Wondering if she and Cavan would have shared one last kiss as well before leaping to their deaths if I hadn't gotten him fired and, in doing so, saved his life.

That night, and many nights after, I tried to write home to Ma about it, but ink never did flow free as blood.

October 31st, 1919, Boston

Somehow, I'd lost my way. I'd kept my hand to the wall the whole time, so whenever there was a fork in the road, I'd kept to the right, hoping the lefts I hadn't taken weren't the only way out. The side of the wall had grown rough, though.

The ground felt just as treacherous, but I'd lost the tracks. Somehow, with the cold and the pain in my ankle and the fear still flitting through my veins, I hadn't noticed the absence of rails beneath my feet right away.

I silently prayed to whoever was still bothering to listen and struck the white phosphorus match. My breath made the flame dance as I breathed a sigh of relief. The light that hadn't killed me cast an otherworldly glow on the walls.

No, not walls. Rocks. These were not the man-made walls of the subway tunnels catacombing through the earth. They were cave sides. No human tool had carved this hollow. It was already here.

My heart drummed in my tightened chest. I broke into a sprint trying to go back the way I'd come, but my ankle shot through with pain. I hobbled back for as long as the match held out, yet could find neither the tracks nor the fork in the road where I'd veered from the path.

I stumbled blindly in the sudden darkness, now even blacker than before. My hand always on the wall. It began to feel moist to the touch. I listened for anything: the sound of the world above me, the thrum of the streets above, even the rhythmic drone of a train would have been reassuring then. Nothing.

I felt a shift in the air whisper against my skin. I struck another match and found myself in a wide cavern with several paths branching off of it. Somehow I'd gotten myself even more turned around. An old glass lantern lay broken on the ground. Someone had been here.

Panic trilled in my ears as my blood sang through the artery on my neck. I was lost. Completely lost. Not even the rats trespassed down here. I had no idea which path I'd come down or which—if any—led out.

For a moment I thought I heard someone. Something halfway between prayer and keening, a mournful, wailing chant. I was past telling myself it was my own echo or an impossible draft and tore down one of the paths as fast as my searing bone would allow.

The air felt cold. For the first time since descending into the T station, it did not hang still and stale. There was a draft. Which meant there was also a way out. Somewhere close. A sudden breeze sent the smoke whispering up in a sinister prayer, my poison match once again plunging me into the abyss.

I took a step and the earth fell out from under me.

Spring 1911, New York City

I held my sign aloft, my arm muscles protesting as fiercely as I was. I was not alone. The streets were clogged with people. Over 140 people had died in the fire, most of them young women trying to support themselves and their families.

Virgin sacrifices to a wealth-hoarding beast. But what wealth it already had in its clutches was never enough, and it was the laborers and the migrant workers and the children working more hours than they had years who were crushed as the fist clutched ever tighter.

Anger coursed through the workers that had powered our industrializing world for years, black circles rippling through the waters on both sides of the Atlantic. Each cave-in at the mines and crumbling factory and poison product was a rock to send the waves out further.

Triangle Shirtwaist had been the spark, outrage catching, blazing, and spreading as fast as the cloth-packed factory itself. So here we were. I felt the energy buzzing around me. Noise everywhere. Roars. Chants. Shouts.

And, for once, it seemed like they were listening. People were talking, not people like Barrow and Uncle Jim and Ma who'd been grumbling mutely for generations, but people who mattered. Laws were going to change. No more would we stand for locked doors and no exits and piles upon piles of cotton tinder nestled about garment workers like kindling.

My heart's mournful elegy rose into the chorus of the masses at the protest. Our hearts beat as one. Our words shouted as one. It was the fight song of a new generation, one far different from the Battle Hymn of the Republic that had come rolling over the county and the country that might have been, but a song just as noble.

My chest swelled with pride, for once easing the guilt and grief and fear that had gripped it since my friends had died. That's when the screams started. Men, angry and shouting. Girls like me were screaming and running from the crowd. The police were there, beating someone back, though whether it was us protesters or the men attacking us I couldn't tell.

That's when the man tore my sign from me. The last thing I saw was his face contorted to scream at me as he swung the sign. My own words splintered as they struck me.

October 31st, 1919, Boston

My cry, shrill as a canary, sang through the echoing black. I tried to stand and my ankle gave way. I couldn't possibly be more afraid, so I didn't bother to hold my breath as I stuck another white phosphorus match. I was in a small tunnel, no doubt naturally occurring.

I looked to where the ground had given way beneath me above. Boston was built on concrete and marshland. I suppose there were only so many passages we could dig beneath the city before the honeycombing holes took their toll.

I eyed something on the wall. On one foot, I managed to lift myself up and stumble over to it. Someone had carved something with a knife that age had worn away. I ran my hand along the cool stone, holding the light closer. There were many messages here. Some in the stone; some in ash; some in ink; some in blood, aged near as brown as the earth.

I saw French, German, Italian, something that might have been Russian, English in a nearly unreadable script. The words "ſtay out" and "my ſins" were the most I could decipher. A French line said something about God. Elsewhere on the wall I found a rough approximation of those winged skulls on old graves, jabbed crudely into the wall by some tool or other. I followed the messages, scrawled in haste and desperation, further down the tunnel.

Had they all died down here, all of them scratching their own epitaphs into the walls of their tomb? If so many had found themselves lost down here, why were there not more bodies? Had they found a way out?

My hand brushed something. A strange pattern on the rock. It was very old, with some kind of paint still clinging in the deeper indentations of the carving. It looked almost like the designs on Indian art.

Must have been. Who else would have carved intricate designs into the heart of an ancient underground labyrinth beneath Boston? No rail worker or lost vagrant would have had paint on them for such an artistic work.

Where on God's green earth was I? Unless I wasn't on God's green earth at all but somewhere else. Somewhere beyond, further in, elsewhere. Something beneath. My grandmother's tales came back to me. My neck needled with sweat.

Something stirred behind me. I whipped my head around and saw nothing. A draft again? Or maybe a rat. I heard a voice. Then footsteps. My heart hammered its own desperate epitaph against my chest.

No, it was nothing. There was no one else down here. Just me and maybe a rat and probably a thousand insects or so. I tried not to think of the worms burrowing into my grave with the same mindless progress of every miner who'd lived and died in Logan County. Always moving forward to enrich the fertile earth for someone else, yet never getting anywhere themselves beyond survival. I pictured spiders and fairies spinning me into my grave, holding me here forever, weaving my own shroud around me as quickly and efficiently as the looms in linen mills.

No. Those were the fancies of a child. I had far too many real things to fear. I turned back to the wall. My fingers traced the carvings. Perhaps there was something here. Some hint of a way out. Surely if this cave was used by Indians they would have had a way in. The T had not always been here. There must have been another way down.

"There has to be a way out," I said aloud.

"Way out. Way out. Way out." The cave walls echoed, taunting me.

I slid to the ground, still holding the lucifer. A sob escaped me and the tension and soreness and fatigue flooded in to take its place. I wished I could wrap myself up in the stolen shawl and hide or, better yet, disappear completely.

"I just want to go home." I pleaded.

To the house with Cavan, to Madam O'Keefe's, to our ramshackle house in Logan County spilling with siblings who were likely grown by now. Any of them would have done.

"Go home. Go home. Go home."

"I just want to go home."

Something about that last echo was wrong. It was my words but someone else's voice. A deeper voice. And not West Virginian at all. It sounded almost...

Irish.

Whatever color I had left drained from me. An arm, equally pale, appeared before my eyes. I glanced up in horror. There stood the Irishman I'd found, very much alive before me.

"Do you need any help, lass?" he asked. "The boys can't be far. We just laid the track. I must have dozed off."

I stared, unable to move or speak, though my heart had words enough for both of us. I could hear it roaring in both ears and I wouldn't have been surprised if the Irishman heard it to.

"I'm trying to get home to my dear old girl and the little ones," he said, handing me the photograph I'd found on him earlier. "Had to come to Boston. There's no work back home. But I told her I'd be home before the hay needs bringing in. Write her every day I do."

"Wh-what are you? Why are you here?"

Confusion washed across his face, leaving a scowl in its wake. He glared down at me.

"What?" he growled. "You're too good to be helped by a mick like me? I do honest work, though I doubt I'll ever see honest pay. What does your husband do? Your da? They can drink themselves to death and whore away their lives all they want, but we paddies are the lecherous drunks? Do you think I want to be here? Do you think I want to lay the railroads to give dirt poor wretches like you a way out while my countrymen drop dead every mile or so? If you want us out of your country so bad, get the damn tyrants out of mine. I'll be glad to go and leave you free of us micks, you Protestant bitch."

He moved as if to strike me. I put up my hand to stop him, the match still held in a death grip in my other hand. My wedding ring gleamed in the light. It was a claddagh. An old heirloom from some Neely relative or other generations back. It had been all Cavan had to offer, though more than I had expected. The Irishman seemed to deflate.

"You're Irish?"

My mouth was still disconnected from the rest of me. I couldn't speak or move. The Irishman's eyes fell on the match in my other hand. He felt his pockets and his bag.

"Or did you steal it off some poor soul's corpse like you did my Lucifers?" he raged, looming over me.

I stumbled back and tried to find my feet. My ankle felt like it had been run through by a knife.

The Irishman grabbed my arm. "You left me here to die and then you pick my body clean. Damn you all. We built the railroads for you. We fought the Mexicans for you. We killed the Indians for you. We cleared this godforsaken country for you and then you push us into the graves we dug."

"I didn't!" I shrieked. "'I'm a miner's daughter. My people died same as yours. We powered the country and made other men rich and we got nothing! There's tyrants in West Virginia too!"

I broke my arm away and bolted as much as my ankle allowed, but my eyes were on the Irishman. I ran into what must have been the cave wall but didn't feel nearly as hard. I turned my head and found myself for the second time that night staring into the face of the immigrant woman.

I screamed so loud I could have woken the dead, had they still lain in the earth like they were supposed to.

Summer 1917, New York City

Barrow's letters had stopped. I kept writing to him, to his Ma, and to Mary Beth Barrow back in Logan County, to anyone who might know what had happened. For months I held onto the hope that he was somewhere too remote or too hostile for mail. Surely, his letters were just lost or slow. There was a war on, after all. Who knew? Maybe he was on some secret mission and couldn't risk a letter.

But each day the hope evaporated a little more, the angel's share of my brewing anguish. The truth cut deeper and deeper into my bones. Homer Barrow was dead. He was never coming home. Never coming back for me, if indeed he had ever meant to at all.

I had no one to cry on the night I finally accepted his death. Kate was gone, the men who'd locked her and all the others in an unventilated scrap pile and let them burn brought to justice. Though truth was you couldn't be half as honest calling it "justice" as Myrtle Kagy had been when she wore her Mama's pure white dress to church for her wedding day.

They'd had to pay seventy-five dollars for each dead girl. Seventy-five dollars that hadn't saved Mickey's life any more than it had soothed Mr. and Mrs. Brannon's grief. One of the men responsible was found locking doors again in the next factory he'd moved on to. They fined him twenty dollars for it.

With Kate gone and no job, Cavan had left. Off to some cousin or other in Boston who might have work for him, if he didn't mind adding a few extra sins to his weekly confession. I had found work where I could. A tannery here. A factory there. I had tried not to think about Kate, but I saw her everywhere. I heard Battista in every laughing girl. Mr. Williams in every foreman and supervisor who looked at me.

My work had gotten sloppy, distracted. My mind was a blur or a blank half as often as not, ever since I'd gotten hit in the head at the protest or maybe since the fire. I couldn't make rent at the boarding house and had had to leave, though not before helping my new roommate obtain an elixir for her womanly troubles, the fifth time a girl in the house had done so since I had moved in (that I knew of, at least).

When I finally accepted that Barrow's letters weren't lost, I gave up pretending to focus. I lost my job as a laundress in a hotel. The windowless hovel I'd been living in since leaving Madam O'Keefe's threw me out on the street.

It was cold that night. The first of many. A man approached more than once, said he had work to offer if I wanted a warm bed and a meal to go with it, so long as I wasn't picky with my taste in men. I refused. The girls I saw take him up on his offer wound up just as cold and hungry when what beauty they had left burned too low. And not all of their scars were invisible.

My grandfather had always said that staying in Logan County would turn your lungs black, but cities would do the same to your heart. I had made my choice. It never occurred to me that the city would poison both.

I didn't know how long it had been since I'd last pulled a crust of moldy bread from the garbage or swiped the milk, blue-veined and poisoned as it was, from an unattended doorstep. I leaned against brick somewhere, my eyes no doubt as hollow as my stomach. As the rest of me, for that matter.

People passed by me all day, quickly averting their eyes or sidestepping me. Those who'd been longer in the city kept their heads down and kept trudging, like a herd of cows against a winter gale. They were smart enough never to have to look away in the first place.

I shrank back when a man approached. Yet, to my surprise, he neither spat on me nor asked me to return the favor of food or money with the only sweet thing not rationed during the war. He didn't even press a coin into my hand and hurry off.

"Are you okay?" he asked, kneeling down to see me.

I stared blankly, uncomprehending.

"Do you have any people left?" he asked. "A ma or a da somewhere?"

"Not here," I croaked.

Even if I had the money to get back home, what prospects did I have left there? I supposed since my sister, Elizabeth, bled out in childbed, there was at least one man in Logan County in need of new wife, but that was hardly worth moving heaven and earth to get home to.

This man had a soothing accent and kind eyes under his drooping hat. Something about him made me feel at ease.

"Have you eaten today?" He seemed genuinely concerned as he searched my face for something.

I said nothing.

"Yesterday?"

I shook my head.

He took off his hat, running his fingers through auburn curls. "Well, let's see if we can't get you something to eat, eh, lassie?"

It hit me slower than it should have. "C-Cavan?"

His eyes went wide. "You know me?"

"Cavan?" I said again, barely letting myself believe it. Hunger and exhaustion and fever on a winter's night beneath a bridge had made me see things before. "Cavan, is it really you?"

"Jesus, Mary, and Joseph," he said. "Lara? Lara Rae Brecken, what happened to you?"

I fainted when he pulled me to my feet. The next I knew I was in the house of some of his old Communist friends, getting ladled soup. When I was able to sit, a woman handed me a stale hunk of bread to sop up what was left.

After that I fell back asleep. Cavan and the woman's husband talked politics as I came in and out, each time sinking into the warm depth of sleep rather than pull myself back to the sharp reality of the living.

They spoke of unions, of the revolution in Russia, of rumblings elsewhere. The man, an oddly educated fellow, kept likening it to the olden times. Something about how people of antiquity had fortified buildings and castles with human sacrifices. Padding the walls with people or laying them to rest in a corner where such an offering would be needed most to ensure that the structure held.

The grander the thing they were building, the greater the sacrifice demanded. Some buildings could do with a peasant or two. Great fortifications sometimes called for princes and nobles.

Everyone knew they could be called upon to die. Any day they could be offered up so that something new could be raised. Society had fed and clothed and kept them. It was only fair they give back, their death the foundation that kept the walls from crumbling away or being breached by enemies.

It was the same here, the man said. Workers had too long been the ones who'd suffered for society's progress. It was only fair that the privileged few pay their dues for once. After all, they were the ones who prospered when the factories went up and the mines went down.

When I finally woke for good, the man was sharing a cigarette with Cavan as the woman scraped supper together. After eating, the woman, a strong-armed farm girl from up North by the name of Mrs. Murray, I came to learn, attacked my hair with a comb. My hair was in a worse state than the Lachey children's after a humid summer in Logan County, but she dug in as stubbornly as our boys in France and refused to let my matted snarls keep their hold.

I thanked them all profusely and Mrs. Murray even washed my clothes along with Mr. Murray's and hers (a kindness to even call them "clothes"). It turned out Cavan had been coming back and forth from New York to Boston on some kind of business for some time.

It had been six years since Kate had died and Cavan was still unmarried. Too busy with his work, he told Mr. Murray, and didn't have much put by to entice a wife anyway. But Mrs. Murray would hear none of his excuses, insisting that with all his family back in Ireland or off in the war, he needed someone to look after him and turn such a sorry excuse for a fit young man into a properly fed, properly groomed husband.

So, seven summers later than I'd planned, I married. I wrote home to tell my family that I was now Mrs. Neely and to inform them that I was moving to Boston. I might as well have told them I'd been a spy for Germany the whole time or that I'd assassinated the Archduke myself on my way home from skipping church. It might have gone better than telling them I'd married an Irish Catholic whose accent had barely dulled and who kept the company of Irish nationalists and Communist Jews.

A few months later I received a letter from Ma wishing me well and saying that it was too bad I couldn't have come home after my brother-in-law ran off, that my nieces would have loved to see me and my wasn't the younger one just the spit and image of my sister. After that, I never heard from any of my family again.

October 31st, 1919, Boston

The immigrant woman stood there, flesh filling out her high cheekbones and her black hair shining as though no dust had every touched it. She held the same bundle in her arms, only now the bundle was filled with a pink and squirming baby instead of a withered little corpse. She stood tall, pride shining like the match light in her face. But that was not the only fire in her eyes.

She took a step toward me, hissing something I did not understand.

"Wh-what do you want with me?" Every part of me was shaking. "Why am I here? Where are we? What did I do?"

With a flash of pure hatred, the woman reached out a bone-thin hand. I shrieked, thinking she would rake the flesh from my bones. Instead she clutched the shawl around me and ripped it away.

"Mine," she said. "Thief."

Shannon Barnsley

"You speak English?" My head was swimming. It had done that here and there since the protest. Lights danced before my eyes until I couldn't tell what direction was up.

"I come here to be safe. Keep children safe." Her words were precise, punctuated by both her accent and her fury. "You take advantage of us. You turn us out. You steal from us. We freeze down here like dog. And then you have nerves to take my shawl from my skeleton. Go to America, they say. There you live in comfort. But even dead I am still only serving yours."

"M-my comfort?" I echoed. "What comfort have I ever had? I'll freeze down here too, you loon! My husband is in prison. My father is dead. All of my friends are dead. My fiancé is dead. My sister is dead. And her children are starving just like yours."

She hugged the shawl to her chest, along with the baby, looking as if she might cry. She hummed a lullaby I had never heard.

"I just want to go home," I prayed.

Even the laundry in the hotel in New York City would have been a paradise right about now. At least it was warm. The clothes drying on the wooden racks, reusing the heat from the engine downstairs. I used to sleep next to it sometimes. I wasn't the only one either.

"I can't go home. My home is gone." She looked up at me again. "And now I am stuck here. We are your ghost. Forever."

She threw herself at me, shrieking like a banshee. I screamed and fought her off, staggering a few steps. I spun to get away, the cave spinning around me. The eyes of the little blonde girl were on me.

"Please?" she held her hand out. "No food today."

I shook my head, backing away, and bumped into yet another impossible apparition. This one was a girl of twelve, maybe thirteen, with mismatched socks and a patched skirt. She had a round, pale face and hair like cornsilk bleached in the sun. Half of it was up in a braided loop. Half had been torn free, along with part of her scalp, temple, and ear.

Her arm hung off in a bloody mash of angles. Bone stuck out of flesh that couldn't possibly be hanging on of its own accord. Beneath her eyes were the purple bags of a factory girl. No doubt she'd gotten caught in the mangle or some other hideous machine.

"Please, Ma'am," she said, "don't fire me. I'll come in Sunday. I will. I'm sorry I asked. I just wanted to go to church. My parents need my pay. I'll work it, I will."

A curly-haired boy spilled out of the darkness. His clothes were blackened and burned and his hair was singed. He coughed like he had the black lung.

"Why did they burn our house?" he asked.

"I- I don't know. I'm sorry."

"Eli and Max got out. They always slept light. I woke up coughing. I tried to follow them, but I fell down. The smoke made my eyes burn. I got so sleepy. When I woke up I was here. Where are we?"

"I don't know. I'm sorry."

The boy began to cry. A young man probably about seventeen in a British uniform appeared behind him. His skin was dark brown and a bayonet stuck through his chest. Another man, barely old enough for the strawberry blonde peach fuzz on his chin, took up the ranks beside him. A railroad spike had been driven through his leg and he coughed blood into a faded woman's handkerchief.

At my side was a middle-aged black woman with deep-set eyes and wringing hands. "Have you seen my boy? My only boy?"

"My daughter!" A woman shrieked. "They came in the night! They took my daughter! Those savages took my eldest girl! Goody Harris's boys were taken same as my girl, my poor Charity."

"What about my husband?" A pregnant woman about my age asked, a toddler latched onto her leg. "He disappeared down at the docks. I haven't seen him since. He could be on a ship halfway around the world by now. Or floating in the harbor. I'll never know."

She sobbed as the child began to wail. Another British soldier pushed past her, his skin tarred and feathered as salt tears stung damaged flesh. His heather brown hair had come loose from its tie and his uniform would never pass muster.

A man with Italian coloring appeared at my other side, his Army uniform spick and span. This uniform was from the war I knew. Before my eyes it transformed into civilian rags. His clean shaven face grew into an unruly beard as his shoe polish black hair matted and was shot through with grey.

"Bread for a soldier?" he asked.

"I don't- I don't h-h-have any," I stuttered, my own accent more apparent.

"You!" A woman my mother's age grabbed my arms. "My boys died fighting you Dixie bastards. Three dead on the battlefield; one deserted, God rest his soul; and my last boy taken by a fever. My five boys! I lost all of them!"

"The war is over," I said. "It's been over a long time. I've lost people in war too."

"So have I," said a girl in Colonial clothing, holding a hoop and stick in one hand and a sibling in the other.

"And me," said a man wearing clothing from sometime in the 19th century.

"And I," said a woman in clothing even older and more out of fashion than the girl's. "The Indians killed my husband for the French."

"The French killed my husband when he fought for the English," said an Indian woman with black hair spilling over a beaded neck. Her English was clearer than my own.

Another woman stepped forward speaking French. An Indian man stepped forward with yet another grievance I couldn't understand but knew all too well.

An Indian child ran screaming through the cavern. He ran right through me, shrieking. An arrow caught him in the shoulder. He fell to the earth and kept falling right through it. All around me swirled the fury of a thousand battles. Muskets. Arrows. Canons echoed deafeningly through the caves. Horses. Red coats. Blue coats. French. Hessians. Indians.

I heard a dog bark somewhere. A woman with a lantern beckoned fugitive slaves to follow her. Another dried the same dish over and over, her late 19th century fashion not enough to cover the bruises. A lunatic cried herself to sleep in chains.

Orphans screamed. Wizened tramps begged. Women screamed curses at the goodwife who had implicated them before dropping to the earth on a noose or being taken away to jail. Midwives covered in blood shook, their eyes wide with shock. Children in the stocks. People shot, run through, stabbed, scalped, drowned, beaten, and left to die, frozen, starved, lost, sold, kidnapped, abandoned.

Maids in torn dresses. Emaciated children covered in chilblains. Widows still waiting for a ship to come in. An Indian boy of sixteen with an antler piercing his belly. Another with a neck crooked near sideways from a fall. Men, women, and children riddled over with smallpox, crying out for help. Trappers shivering, unable to find their way. An Irishman beaten bloody and robbed. A Polish man with a flag around his neck as a noose.

An apprentice run ragged by his master. A young woman screaming for her dead children. An old woman spinning mindlessly on her wheel as tears ran silently down her face. A mulatta girl with sad eyes.

A young man in a British uniform cheering victory before suddenly aging before her. Now he wore a hodgepodge Yankee uniform. He held his comrade as they both bled out. A man desperately looking for the wife he'd left at the homestead. A quadroon muttering revenge he'd never take.

A street urchin tried to pick my pocket as a drunkard raved in my ear. A minister was having a breakdown a few feet away. A woman with silvering hair pushed past him, shouting her wares with growing desperation. A child with porcupine quills all over her face and no idea where mother was. An Indian man in English finery jostled the countless others nearby trying to reach me.

They screamed and jeered and begged and prayed and shouted. Children pulled at my skirt. So many children. My chest was tight. I couldn't get air. Was there even enough air down here?

Blacksmiths. Farmers. Merchants. Cobblers. Businessmen. Brewers. Innkeepers. Furniture makers. Navy officers. Wheelwrights. Factory workers. Mill workers. Servants. Slaves. They were in every color and clothing and creed, from Quakers to Spaniards to German Catholics to Portuguese whalers to Lutherans and Calvinists to prisoners from Europe stripped of their titles and bound for the Americas to penniless poets and political upstarts.

"And what airs do you think you're puttin' on?" a woman said behind me. She was clearly a prostitute. "Think you're better than us? That we weren't just like you a few years ago?"

I could feel the sweat on my lip and palms.

"Think you're special? That our lot will never be yours?" the prostitute asked. "That you're different and things'll turn out okay because God loves you? Well, our mothers said God loved us too and we wound up where we are all the same. You're nothing special. You're nothing at all."

They were everywhere. So many lost souls all trapped down in the underbelly beneath Boston. Eternity caught in my throat as I choked down panic. I closed my eyes.

"This isn't real," I said. Heat flushed through my core, making my numb arms suddenly feverish. "I'm not here. This isn't real. This isn't real. This isn't real."

"Real. Real. Real."

I screeched at the top of my lungs. A shrill sound that grew into a primal scream.

The voices all around, threatening to consume whatever remained of my sanity were suddenly gone. I breathed, trying to quell my terror as it bubbled over. I opened my eyes and saw only the cave. The ghosts had vanished, back to the ashes and shadows and worn graves from whence they came.

I was alone.

"You were always alone, Lara," the voice said behind me.

I tried running. The pain screamed through my bones, but it was no louder than my fear. Footsteps echoed in the cave.

"You don't have to be alone. I'll take care of you. I'm the only one who ever will. Your family, Barrow, Cavan, they never loved you. Who could love someone like you? You're a burden to everyone. You've always been a burden. Why do you think they were all so glad to be rid of you?"

The footsteps quickened their pace behind me but did not run. They did not need to. A brisk pace was more than enough to catch me in my crippled state.

"You're one of us, Lara. We love you. We're your real family. We'll never leave you."

I would have screamed, but there was no point. No one could hear me down here. Wherever here was. My match fell to the ground and I stumbled, cutting my hands on the rock beneath as I tried to catch myself.

Something cool touched my arm. A hand, white as bone in the flickering light. Light that shouldn't have been coming from the fallen match, but I couldn't imagine where else it would be. I could make out a face floating above mine. Or perhaps below. I couldn't tell anymore.

The face stared down at me. Eyes bluer than cornflower, features sharp as a cat's and fine as a doe's, hair in near-white wisps fine as dandelion fluff and shining with the sheen of a beaver hat newly slicked with quicksilver. Milk white skin run through with blue veins.

At first I wasn't sure if it was a man or a woman, though I suppose either way it wasn't entirely accurate. Whatever was before me, it wasn't human. For all its delicate beauty, something about the creature made me certain he was male.

The old stories were true. In a way, all stories are.

—

"Need some help, Lara?" he asked, his voice like an echo lilting a prayer, or perhaps a lover's sigh.

Fall 1919, Boston

It was Gate Night, the night before All Hallows' Eve. Distant memories of the old stories nagged at me. During All Hallows' Eve the veil between the world of the living and the world beyond was lifted. Our world and their world all blurred together like ink running on a page in my old primer when we schoolgirls would try to run home in the rain, shrieking and splashing up mud all the way.

Gate Night was when the veil began to thin. Things bleeding through in the corners or fading in and out. I wondered if Cavan believed that or if he'd left the old tales back across the ocean when he'd come to America.

I stood, match in hand, as the gas sputtered into life. Cavan was in the other room. Since the war for independence had broken out back in Ireland, he had had quite a bit more "business" going back and forth between Boston and New York.

He never told me exactly what it was he did. On good days I believed that it was to protect me. The less I knew, the safer I was. On bad days, I worried he just didn't trust me enough. Though Cavan never said, I knew he was helping move something and bringing it to men who could smuggle it into Ireland and into IRA hands. My guess was guns, but I couldn't be sure.

Apparently, the police could.

I heard the door smash open as they stormed in. I heard the shouting. I ran to the room, my heart in my throat. Cavan was on his hands and knees on the floor, wincing in pain. Six policemen had swarmed the house.

"Lara, run!" Cavan shouted.

I didn't pretend to be a heroic romantic. I ran. Two officers followed me as the others arrested Cavan. I was out the back door, through the loose board in the fence, down into the neighbor's cellar, and out to the street on the other side before they could say "Steely Boys."

I hadn't done anything, but if Cavan was gunrunning for the IRA that wasn't just smuggling. It was aiding terrorism. If they thought I was in any way involved, or just had reason to pretend I was involved, it wouldn't end well for me and certainly wouldn't make things any better for Cavan.

If the cops had come for Cavan, though, none of his friends or "business partners" were safe to go to and neither were their wives and sisters. I had nowhere to go, no one else to turn to. Once again I was one lost girl with no education, skills, prospects, or connections in a great big city far from Logan County.

So, I ran. And kept running.

October 31st, 1919, Boston

"How do you know my name?"

The hand on my arm was cool as the rock. On closer inspection, the man seemed to be wearing some kind of formal attire, the kind that had gone out of fashion long, long ago. His white-blonde hair was long, held back in an elaborate array of foam-white cascades.

"I can help you, Lara," he said. "Come home with me. It's warm here. You'll never be hungry here."

I knew enough of old world tales to know that accepting food sealed whatever doom lay in store.

"We have sweetmeats and tarts from every berry in this world and a few more besides." His slightly pointed teeth shone like pearls in the dun-colored underworld around me. "And the wine, oh, the wine. Like you've never had in your life. You'll dance all night and still hear it singing in your veins come morning."

"What do you want from me?" I asked.

His paper white finger traced my cheek. "Nothing the world above hasn't already taken. Your youth, your health, your beauty, your strength. Your spirit."

I tried to get away, but there was nowhere to go and attempting to stand made my head swim with pain. I leaned against the wall to avoid falling. The bodies. The dead. The words on the wall.

This man was no angel come to deliver me. Hades. Fairyland. Tir Na nOg. Helheim. The spirit world. Whatever realm he beckoned me to was not one I was like to return from.

"Come."

A chill ran through the tunnel. Now I didn't even have a stolen death shroud to wrap about me. My torn sleeves were red with blood. My freckled olive skin was patterned over in yellow and purple bruises and covered in gooseflesh.

"Come with me, little mortal," he said. "Come home with me."

There was no way out. Nothing to grab hold of or run to or defend myself with.

"Leave it all behind. There's nothing up there for you. No one wants you up there. No one loves you up there. But we will. Just come with me. I'll take care of you. We'll be your family. You can be free, Lara."

He pulled a crisp apple from somewhere in his coat. His too-sharp teeth bit down on it with a crunch more satisfying than Tom Sawyer ever could have managed after he lured the other boys in to do his work for nothing more than the pleasure of it. Juices ran down his chin, his lips slick with tart sweetness.

He offered it to me. "Want a bite, Lara?"

Hesitantly, I took the apple. Green and red. It smelled sweeter than any apple pie that ever wafted in any window in Logan County. It was just as good as I imagined. Biting into it was like tasting a memory of a day spent picking apples from a sun-dappled tree in some perfect corner of America I had never seen.

I smiled nervously as he grinned at me. I lowered the hand that held the apple. Juice ran down my palm, bleeding onto my fingers. He held his hand out to me.

"Come."

I let go of the wall and took it. He pulled me back up to full height, which was about the same as his. My ankle did not give way. I felt no pain. In fact, I felt nothing at all.

Winter 1921, Logan County, West Virginia

No one spoke to me. They just stared, solemn-eyed, as I came limping into town, queerly dressed and bold as you please, without so much as a word of explanation to my name. Still, despite the silence, the news spread like Spanish Flu through the now even poorer and more sparsely populated town I had once called home.

By the time I reached my house, Aunt Betsy, or a woman half a foot too short and much too thinly-haired to be Aunt Betsy but who claimed her title all the same, was there in the snow-patched yard. Her mouth fell open at the sight of me.

"Lara Rae?" she asked.

I nodded.

She moved as if to hug me but recoiled at the coldness of my touch and the silvered glint shining in my eye. Still, I was her kin. I saw two girls standing in the doorframe. They looked like pale, thin echoes of my sister. My older brother, Johnnie, and my little brothers and sisters were nowhere to be seen. Neither was my mother.

Aunt Betsy ushered me in to offer a cup of black coffee thick as tar and barely hot enough to warm the tin cup, let alone my hands.

"Where on earth have you been, child?" she asked, keeping an arm's distance from me, as though I were something too alien to fully accept back into her home.

I wanted to tell her. But how could I? How could I tell her of what I had been through, how I had been swallowed up by the city's underbelly and held for two years—what felt like two hundred there—in an underworld of shadow and silver tongues whose promises burned bright as embers but turned to ash the moment I tried to warm the lifeblood back into my numbly beating heart?

How could I tell her how I'd bided my time? How I'd played my part without a trace of guile for so long, until the chance was finally there. My fey captor finally let down his guard. And without so much as a shadow's lingering regret, I was gone.

I'd walked right out of his grand hall and emerged from the mouth of a cave near a farm in Pennsylvania. I don't know why the door to the world below spat me out three states away anymore than I knew how I'd gotten down there in the first place. I didn't even know what state or year I was in until I stole a paper off a traveling druggist I met on the road.

Were there doors to the other side dotting all over the country, or just in places like Boston's underground, where so many lost souls had passed through and never found their way out? Did all the great cities have them? Rome and Babylon and Jerusalem and London and Paris? Did the doors shut when the cities were sacked and overgrown or remain like old standing stones, as quiet testaments to the secrets and sins of the past?

Whatever the reasons behind the doors, I'd finally found myself back on the side of the living. I'd kept walking—my limp returned the moment I stepped back into the sun—until I reached Logan County.

"My husband was a gunrunner for the IRA. The police took him away and I never saw him again. I couldn't go to his friends after that and their wives never did take kindly to an Orange hussy ensnaring a good Catholic lad like Cavan. I had no choice but to seek hospitality in a...home for fallen women." It was a manner of truth, I supposed. "I've thought of nothing but home every day since."

The two rail-thin girls stared at me with wide blue eyes as Aunt Betsy absorbed my tale.

Finally, I could bear it no longer. "Aunt Betsy, what on earth happened here?" There had been nothing in town but children too weary to bother looking hungry anymore and folk bleaker than the ones I left, with even more mistrust in their eyes. "Where's Ma? And Johnnie? And the rest?"

"Your brother's in jail. For treason. As for the little ones, Annie married Wilbur Lachey. He died in the war, but she has a baby girl. She just remarried. One of John Massie's boys. Becky drowned in the creek at nine years old and Milly, God forgive her, Milly threw herself on the railroad tracks after her husband, Lee Gibson, died in the battle along with Hank and Jesse." There was a catch in her throat as she said my little brothers' names. "And Jasper, little Jasper, he died in the riot. A policeman shot him. What kind of a man shoots a boy of twelve, I'll never know."

It was strange to think of Jasper as anything but a baby. He'd been two when I left. Hank and Jesse in a battle seemed just as ridiculous. They were nothing but balls of snot, drool, and energy in my failing memory. Had they gone to war? Had they died in France like Barrow? Were they even old enough to enlist? Hank would have been, I supposed, but Jesse couldn't have been more than sixteen even if he were alive today.

"And Ma?" I asked.

"Your Ma died of a broken heart," she said. "It was the same with Mrs. Barrow after Homer died in the battle."

"Bet he gave those German bastards hell first."

Aunt Betsy went pale. "Oh, dear. No. Homer didn't die in the war in Europe. He went missing and his Ma near gave up hope. But then she got the letter from a hospital in Boston. He'd been injured and too disoriented to know up from down. Poor boy didn't even know his own name. When he started to remember, they sent him back home. It's funny, he said he could have sworn he saw you on the street one night. Said you were there one minute and vanished into thin air the next."

"W-what?"

"Nonsense, of course. They said it was probably just him sorting out his memories and his mind playing tricks on him." Aunt Betsy was oblivious to the war drum in my chest. "His Ma was so happy, God rest her soul. But I guess the war never left him and he couldn't leave it. He died in a battle first chance he got. The one on Blair Mountain. Fightin' for the union men from Mingo."

I went cold as she spoke. Russia. Ireland. Not even West Virginia had been spared the wildfire of long-burning resentments that had blazed into war. Revolution was in the air, but it wasn't enough to clear the coal from our lungs. Or to free us from the rusted chains that bound us to the mines, to the railroads they powered, to the roaring dragon of thick, black coal at the heart of America's engine of progress.

Ten thousand miners, she said. Against three thousand. For once the odds were in their favor. Until President Harding sent in the Army. The very army that boys like Barrow had bled with already, fighting for a country they suddenly found on the other side of the barrel.

They'd bombed us in the end, Aunt Betsy told me. Mines burning and guns smoking as they buried us myth-deep in the earth, along with the rest of their shame (and more than a Cherokee or two). Guns and bombs meant for our enemies in the war overseas had instead been turned on Americans who'd dared to defy the coal company in Logan County.

But it wasn't just us. Hopes of Peace, Land, Bread that once rose in steaming breaths against the cold Russian air now did little to keep them warm. Just as all of Churchill's efforts to appease the Irish did little to make up for the potatoes they'd gone without, blighted black as our lungs. A treaty had been signed in the end but not the one they had wanted. Once again Ireland had been split in two, the invaders claiming the top, the rest had been made to be content with what lay below.

America had fared better. We'd come out of a decade of war stronger than before, factories and banks had built an assembly line of prosperity that sent money tumbling into the hands of the nouveau-riche. Still, the newly built summer homes in Newport and Great Neck were all well and good for those lucky enough to have climbed the fire escape of upward mobility. It meant nothing to the evicted, unionized families now in shanty-towns all across Southern West Virginia, their tents a festering pox on the backbone of the nation.

Sure, the latest fashions graced the soulless mannequins on the streets of Manhattan, bedecked in increasingly short-skirts as they beckoned foreign girls to the faceless luxuries of the American Dream. But all the linen in the factory that had taken my friend's life wasn't enough to bandage the wounds my fiddler had come home with.

They say he died in the rebellion in September, gone down in a blaze of gun-smoke and glory, but that's a lie. Homer Barrow died on a frozen field in France. All they'd shot that day was a broken spirit in an empty shell, a ghost set free in a puff of smoke.

Breadlines and battle lines criss-crossed the world, binding the victims of the cleansing fires, tributes the new world would be built upon. A necessary sacrifice to remake the surface of the land.

My heart, unwarmed by the fire of my childhood home, sank. I had thought by surviving, by escaping, by keeping my head down against the gales that chilled so many orphans and widows and haunted soldiers that I had somehow avoided my fate. I hadn't. I had only prolonged it. Kate. Cavan. Barrow. I was no less a sacrifice than they had been.

But my sacrifice would not be in vain. I would not go quietly into the dark chapters of history, swept into the shadows to keep our country's legacy clean. I had nothing left to give but myself. My last spark of life.

And with that spark I would watch them all burn. I would be a phoenix rising. And from the ash and coal I would leave in my wake, something new would arise. Though what rose in the shadow of Blair Mountain would be the responsibility of the little girls here with me and the other children of Logan County. All I could do was blow the damn mountain to hell and hope its destruction was enough to leave a blank canvas for those who came after.

"I always hoped you'd find your way back to us," Aunt Betsy said. "I prayed every night for the Good Lord to keep you. And he did."

"Beggin' your pardon, Aunt Betsy," I replied as though commenting on the weather, "but it weren't the Good Lord who kept me."

I set down my cup with the clink of a silver fey bell and rose from the chair. I thanked Aunt Betsy and walked right out the door. Snow was falling now, though for all I knew it was the ashes of the men they'd bombed.

I felt the matchbox in my pocket, a single white phosphorus match still inside. Every night in the hell I'd lived in beneath the city I'd felt the weight of that match. I had needed only to put the match in my mouth and its poison tip would spirit me away for good. But every night I had stayed my hand.

I walked past the ramshackle homes, smaller and dirtier than the coops of the thousand turkey farms I'd passed on my way here. The white-spotted forest welcomed me as a winter wind keened through the trees. How many of them still held guns stashed by the pro-union fighters? Would those guns rust away to nothing or would men take them up again as another wave of anger crashed on the rocks into which we carve our history?

I passed a frozen river with a bone picked clean as a Christmas turkey sticking halfway out of the ice. The water still swirled beneath the silver lining of ice on the surface. I wondered if the bone was Jesse's or Hank's. Barrow's maybe or Lee Gibson's. Strange as it was, I felt nothing at the thought.

My limp kept my pace slow, but even a slow march to battle will get there eventually. By the time the sun hung low in the smoke-colored sky—which was always far too early in coal country—the mountain loomed above me.

It looked innocent enough, covered over with leaves and blanketed in brown needles. But I saw in it a blackness that had always been there. Blair Mountain was seamed through with coal. And I would send that sleeping dragon roaring its death throes into the bleak shroud above me. A beacon lit for all to see, though what message they'd see in it was their business, not mine.

I walked past the threshold of frost-eaten timber into a cold mountain in Logan County as generations of my forebears had before me. I followed the twisting black scars to their source. And with no witness but my own shadow, I took out the match.

Yet before I could strike it, a man grabbed my arm, twisting my little unburnt offering from my hands. I screamed for all I was worth, but a bloodless hand clamped over my mouth. I bit down and pulled away. It wasn't the fey folk this time. It was only men.

The coal miners stood before me, going back as far as I could see. An endless chain I'd tried so hard to break. I would never be free of them. No matter where I went there were ghosts and these were mine.

"What? Too good for us?" taunted a woman with a face older than her years. "Lara Rae always dreaming of fancy folk. Did you have tea with the Astors in New York City?"

"Milly?" I realized with horror.

"You used have tea parties with me," she said. "Always looked up to you, I did. But when I needed you, you weren't here."

"Milly, I-"

"Think you're better than us, do you?" a young man with a string bean build asked.

He might have been Lee Gibson, but I'd been gone too long to recognize half the faces here. I knew they looked like Logan County folk. Lacheys and Kagys and McNabbs. But the names and individuals all blurred.

"No," I said. "No. I just wanted something more than this."

"And why should you get more?" an old man spat. "Young folks these days with their heads in the clouds. I found work in the mine at half your age and I was damn lucky to get it. You young people expect the world on a silver platter. Don't know the meanin' of hard work. It all comes so easy now."

I shook my head.

A girl in my old boots and one of Milly's old dresses skipped past me, singing a ditty about sailing far away. "I'm gonna get out too," she said. "Just like Liza and Milly always said you did."

I felt a stab in my heart at her words. Becky. Sweet little Becky. My baby sister. Elizabeth appeared behind her and wrapped an arm around the girl.

"We needed you," she said.

"I just wanted to get out," I whimpered.

Elizabeth grabbed me. "I never got out. None of us ever get out."

"Think we didn't dream of getting out of the mine?" asked a man with a hunched back. "School always came easy to me. Said I could be something, they did. A shopkeep. A businessman. Even a schoolteacher if I wanted. But Ginny needed the operation and the roof was leaking. Ain't nobody got time for school when their people can't afford milk."

"I kept telling myself I'd put enough by and move my old girl someplace decent."

"I was gonna go out West and strike it rich."

"I did get out. I come home to take care of my younger siblings when Mam and Pap died."

"I swore every day I'd never go down in the mine."

"And me."

"And me."

"And me."

"Me. Me. Me," the cave echoed.

"Nobody survives Logan County. We're all just ghosts on borrowed time."

A man with a pocket watch stepped forward, along with two policemen. They'd been in the coal company's employ. Even they had died here. Soldiers trickled out of the mountain's secret corners. Rebels I recognized and some from Mingo I didn't stood shoulder to shoulder with them in death.

Here they were. All the souls who would never be free of Blair Mountain, haunting it as it had haunted them all their lives. And I was right. There was far more than a Cherokee or two.

That's when Barrow stepped forward, gun in hand. His humble clothes were stained with blood.

"I didn't know it was you," I told him. "We could have run away together. Away from the war and Boston and this godforsaken place."

"No." He shook his head. "We couldn't have. It was always just a dream, Lara."

"Play your fiddle?" I asked. "One more time?"

Barrow shook his head.

"You're one of us," said Jesse.

"You're a West Virginia girl," said Hank. "You belong to the mountain. We all do."

"Ain't no use fighting," said Henry McNabb.

"Nobody ever gets out alive," said the necktied figure of Mr. Barrow.

"Didn't I tell you never to forget where you come from?" said a voice I'd not heard in years. "You're Lara Rae Brecken of Logan County."

"Pa?"

"There's been Breckens in Logan County since some poor fool tenant farmer left Ireland for a better life," said Uncle Jim. "And there's been poor fool tenant farmers in Ireland since some poor fool left Scotland for a better life. The poor fools leavin' West Virginia for California and New York City and Alaska and Chile and Brazil ain't any different."

"But we could change it. We could fight back."

"We tried," said a boy who had to be Jasper, his voice still cracking with youth.

"There has to be a way out," I insisted.

"I'm sorry, Lara," said Barrow. "It was a good dream while it lasted. But that's just fairy stories."

The very mountain shook around me. A cave-in, they'd say. Nothing more. And I'm sure they'd think it was a rock loosed from the ceiling that killed me, instead of something far heavier taking me back down beneath the earth we'd never own. That is, if they found me at all.

But the match remained. My last act a chance that lingered through the seasons I would never live to see. A single match lying in wait for a spark. I had failed to strike a blow, but I had left a poison-tipped weapon poised to strike the heart of the dragon slumbering beneath Blair Mountain.

THE END

Shannon Barnsley is a writer, poet, and folklore devotee from New Hampshire, currently living in Brooklyn. She holds a degree in Creative Writing/Mythology & Religion from Hampshire College. Since graduating she has been found giving tours at an 18th century Shaker village museum, translating English English into American English for a publishing company, and wandering in the woods.

Rebecca Johnson has a B.A. in Creative Writing from California State University, Northridge and is currently continuing her writing education at Chapman University. She is a Los Angeles native and self-acknowledged starving artist. Her love of literature began early in life and stirred her over active imagination, inspiring her to become a writer herself. When she's not writing she's telling herself she should be. She doesn't have a backup plan.

Mariya Suzuki was born in Nara and studied illustration in Long Beach, California. She currently works as an illustrator in Tokyo.

She has contributed her work for many musicians, food professionals and publishers from around the world. Aside from work, she enjoys going around town to draw subjects whose shape or story catches her attention.